I Love You Already!

Jory John & Benji Davies

HarperCollins *Children's Books*

First published by HarperCollins Children's Books,
a division of HarperCollins Publishers, USA, in 2015
First published in hardback in Great Britain by HarperCollins Children's Books in 2015
First published in paperback in 2016

1 3 5 7 9 10 8 6 4 2

ISBN: 978-0-00-816598-7

HarperCollins Children's Books is a division of HarperCollins Publishers Ltd.

Text copyright © Jory John 2015
Illustrations copyright © Benji Davies 2015

Typography by Jeanne L. Hogle

Visit our website at www.harpercollins.co.uk

Printed and bound in China

This book is dedicated to
my great friend, Bill Olin.
—Jory John

For my one true love, Nina
—Benji Davies

"Ahh, I really love spending lazy weekend mornings around my house."

"A morning stroll would be nice. I wonder what ol' Bear is up to."

"Ahhhhhh. Perfect. I have everything I need to spend a pleasant day by myself."

"Bear! It's *Duck*! From next door! Open up! C'mon, buddy!"

"What is it, Duck? I'm busy."

"You don't *look* busy! Besides, we're going for a walk, friend. No arguments. Chop-chop!"

"We can spend some
quality time together."

"No."

"I'll tell you my life's story."

"No."

"You'll tell me *your* life's
story?"

"No."

"We'll get some exercise."

"No."

"We'll look at the clouds."

"No."

"I'll tell you my life's story."

"You already said that."

"But maybe you'll *like* me more..."

"I like you *already*, Duck."

"I'm not taking no for an answer, Bear. We're having fun, whether you want to or not."

"Ugh."

"Take a look around, Bear! Who wants to be alone on a day like this?"

"Me."

"Nonsense!"

"Would you like an ice pop, Bear?"

"I suppose. . ."

"Um, Bear, I might need to borrow a little money."

(Grrr.)

"The absolute best morning you've ever had?"

"No."

"Pleasant?"

"You already said that."

"I just want you to like me, Bear."

"I LIKE YOU ALREADY!"

"But I also like quiet time *by myself.*

If you need me, I'll be relaxing by that tree.

"Now *this* is pleasant. Yes."

"Psst! Bear!!"

"You don't even like me, do you, Bear?"

**"Nonsense. You're basically my family.
I *love* you already, Duck!"**

"Really?
You mean it, Bear?
Do you?
You do?
Huh?"

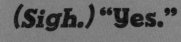

(Sigh.) "Yes."

"That's such good news, Bear! Now we can go on morning walks together, *every single day!* How fun! How perfect! Especially because we live right next door to each other. I always know where to find you!"

"Oh . . . great."

"So . . . you want to see me run really fast, Bear?"

"No."

"Juggle five apples?"

"No."

"Swim across this lake?"

"No."